P9-EFI-169

TIME TRAIN

BY PAUL FLEISCHMAN
ILLUSTRATIONS BY CLAIRE EWART

A Charlotte Zolotow Book
An Imprint of HarperCollinsPublishers

For Jenna
P. F.

For Jules and Jim, Kelly and Nick
C. E.

TIME TRAIN

Text copyright © 1991 by Paul Fleischman
Illustrations copyright © 1991 by Claire Ewart
Printed in the U.S.A. All rights reserved.
Typography by Elynn Cohen
1 2 3 4 5 6 7 8 9 10
First Edition

Library of Congress Cataloging-in-Publication Data
Fleischman, Paul.
    Time train / by Paul Fleischman ; illustrated by Claire Ewart.
        p.   cm.
    "A Charlotte Zolotow book."
    Summary: A class takes a field trip back through time to observe
living dinosaurs in their natural habitat.
    ISBN 0-06-021709-X. — ISBN 0-06-021710-3 (lib. bdg.)
    [1. Dinosaurs—Fiction.   2. Time travel—Fiction.   3. School
excursions—Fiction.] I. Ewart, Claire, ill. II. Title.
PZ7.F59918Ti   1991   90-27357
[E]—dc20   CIP
                                                            AC

TIME TRAIN

"Where to?" the ticket seller asked.

"Dinosaur National Monument," Miss Pym, our teacher, replied. "In Utah."

"That'll be Gate 44. The *Rocky Mountain Limited*." The man counted out eight tickets. "What takes you out West?"

"A field trip for spring vacation," I spoke up. "We want to learn all about dinosaurs."

The man's eyebrows jumped. "In that case, you want the *Rocky Mountain Unlimited*. Gate 44A. And hurry!"

We just made the train as it pulled out of New York. By the time we reached Philadelphia, we knew we were in for an unusual trip.

In Pittsburgh we picked up some new passengers.

In Ohio Miss Pym demanded to speak to the engineer, but he was busy.

At night the con-
ductor handed out
blankets. In the
morning we noticed
that the weather had
changed.

Dinner that evening
was surprisingly good.

By the next morning the weather had warmed up quite a bit.

That afternoon we got off at our stop.

We couldn't find the Green River Motor
Lodge, so we settled for a patch of dry ground
nearby.

In the morning we
saw our first dinosaur.

Emily and Alexander decided to do their project on it. The rest of us fixed scrambled egg for breakfast.

I decided to study stegosaurus eating habits.

Every afternoon
we came back to
our camp and went
swimming or played
ball.

Stuart got some great photographs of the area.

We were having such a good time that we
hardly noticed the days passing. Then one
morning Miss Pym heard a whistle.

It was the *Rocky Mountain Unlimited*, making
its return trip.

Back in New York, my father met me at the
station. "See any dinosaurs?" he joked.
"One or two," I replied.